My Uncle and Me

Copyright © 2018 Ashley Hinds

First edition

ISBN: 978-1-5272-2106-2

For enquiries and multiple book purchases please contact
using the details below.

www.ashleyhindswhdb.com   info@ashleyhindswhdb.com

Acknowledgements

I would like to thank every person reading this book.
I've worked hard to achieve a big dream and I hope you
can do the same. Thank you to God, my wife, family
and friends who have continuously supported me
on this journey to becoming an author.
I also thank my loving nephew who inspired me
to write this book.

Ashley Hinds.
'Work Hard Dream Big'

My Uncle and Me

MUMMY

ME

UNCLE

NANNY

My uncle is my mummy's brother,
my nanny is my mummy's mother.
This book is about my uncle and me,
my family love me like no other.

My uncle was there when I was born,
my crying reminded him of
a thunder storm.

When he is at our house we play game
after game, alphabet and numbers
to give me a big brain.

My mummy sometimes calls me uncle's name, but we are two different people, we are not the same.

They say to him I look like him,
but I do not think he looks like me.

He makes me smile whenever I see him,
at home or in the car, wherever it may be.

I am young and he is old, older than me.
When he goes to work, I go to nursery.

He takes me swimming
and in the water we play,
we splash, we kick
and laugh all day.

At the park we swing, slide and spin, spending time with my uncle is my favourite thing.

When I am at nanny's my uncle pops
his head in, he is oh so funny
he keeps me smiling.

Something strange happened the other day, nanny called me uncle's name, but we are two different people, we are not the same.

At dinner it gets messy,
food falls by my feet,
my uncle always sweeps up
he likes everything neat.

His house, his car and even his shoes,
he has them all in a neat line ready
to choose.

When I go to his house,
I put my shoes down to join the line,
all of his shoes are so much
bigger than mine.

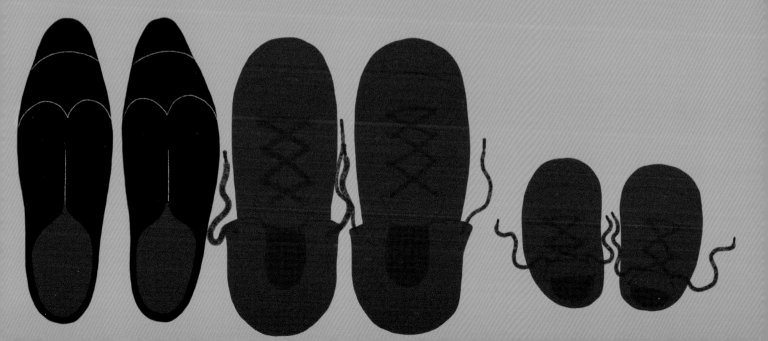

Sometimes my uncle likes quiet,
but I like lots of noise, he reads his books
quietly, while I play with all my toys.

In the garden,
we play in the sunshine,
he throws me up in the air,
we always have a fun time.

I love my uncle and my uncle loves me,
yes I do think we look the same
would you agree?

Even though we look the same,
in so many other ways we are not,
can you remember how we are different
or have you forgot?

Now if people get mixed up and call you
someone else's name, remember to tell them
we are two different people, we are not the same!